For my priceless PBJeebies: Janee, Jessica, and Tammi —K.N.

To my mom: Thank you for all the great costumes —J.F.

Farrar Straus Giroux Books for Young Readers
An imprint of Macmillan Publishing Group, LLC
120 Broadway, New York, NY 10271

Text copyright © 2020 by Kim Norman
Pictures copyright © 2020 by Jay Fleck
Printed in China by RR Donnelley Asia Printing Solutions Ltd., Dongguan City, Guangdong Province
Designed by Aram Kim
First edition, 2020
10 9 8 7 6 5 4 3 2 1

mackids.com

Library of Congress Cataloging-in-Publication Data is available.
ISBN: 978-0-374-31213-8

Our books may be purchased in bulk for promotional, educational, or business use.
Please contact your local bookseller or the Macmillan Corporate and Premium Sales Department at
(800) 221-7945 ext. 5442 or by email at MacmillanSpecialMarkets@macmillan.com.

THE GHOSTS WENT FLOATING

KIM NORMAN

Pictures by
JAY FLECK

Farrar Straus Giroux
New York

The ghosts went floating, one by one,

BOO-rah! BOO-rah!

when Halloween had just begun.

BOO-rah! BOO-rah!

The ghosts went floating, one by one.

The skeletons rattled and joined the fun,

and they all marched up the hill,
in the chill,
by the light of the moon,
moon, moon, moon.

The witches cackled, two by two,

BOO-rah! BOO-rah!

while whipping up a bubbly brew.

BOO-rah! BOO-rah!

The witches cackled, two by two.

They cranked their motors and off they flew,

and they all swept up the hill,

in the chill,

by the light of the moon,

moon, moon, moon.

The mummies stumbled, three by three,

BOO-rah! BOO-rah!

their tattered fabric flying free.

BOO-rah! BOO-rah!

The mummies stumbled, three by three.

Their murmurs echoing frightfully,

and they all limped up the hill,
in the chill,
by the light of the moon,
moon, moon, moon.

The werewolves wandered, four by four.

BOO-rah! BOO-rah!

They howled at each and every door.

BOO-rah! BOO-rah!

The werewolves wandered, four by four.

They crashed the carts at the grocery store,

and they all stalked up the hill,

in the chill,

by the light of the moon,

moon, moon, moon.

The zombies lumbered, five by five,

BOO-rah! BOO-rah!

along a dark and winding drive.

BOO-rah! BOO-rah!

The zombies lumbered, five by five.

You'd never guess that they weren't alive,

and they all lurched up the hill,

in the chill,

by the light of the moon,

moon, moon, moon.

The goblins galloped, six by six,

BOO-rah! BOO-rah!

while waving clubs and pointy sticks.

BOO-rah! BOO-rah!

The goblins galloped, six by six.

They dragged their knuckles on

sidewalk bricks,

and they all trooped up the hill,

in the chill,

by the light of the moon,

moon, moon, moon.

The vampires hovered, seven by seven.

BOO-rah! BOO-rah!

They swooped and looped in seventh heaven.

BOO-rah! BOO-rah!

The vampires hovered, seven by seven,

as clocks and belfries chimed eleven,

and they all flapped up the hill,

in the chill,

by the light of the moon,

moon, moon, moon.

The ghouls went drooling, eight by eight,

BOO-rah! BOO-rah!

erupting from a sewer grate.

BOO-rah! BOO-rah!

The ghouls went drooling, eight by eight,

'cause Halloween is their favorite date,

and they all swarmed up the hill,

in the chill,

by the light of the moon,

moon, moon, moon.

The monsters plodded, nine by nine,

BOO-rah! BOO-rah!

while chased by Dr. Frankenstein.

BOO-rah! BOO-rah!

The monsters plodded, nine by nine.

They staggered in a jagged line,

and they all stomped up the hill,

in the chill,

by the light of the moon,

moon, moon, moon.

The crowd paraded, ten by ten,

BOO-rah! BOO-rah!

and tramped in time like army men.

BOO-rah! BOO-rah!

The crowd paraded, ten by ten.

They turned a corner and stopped...

What then?

And they all flocked UP YOUR STREET...